A NOTE TO PARENTS

Reading Aloud with Your Child

Research shows that reading books aloud is the single most valuable support parents can provide in helping children learn to read.

- Be a ham! The more enthusiasm you display, the more your child will enjoy the book.
- Run your finger underneath the words as you read to signal that the print carries the story.
- Leave time for examining the illustrations more closely; encourage your child to find things in the pictures.
- Invite your youngster to join in whenever there's a repeated phrase in the text.
- Link up events in the book with similar events in your child's life.
- If your child asks a question, stop and answer it. The book can be a means to learning more about your child's thoughts.

Listening to Your Child Read Aloud

The support of your attention and praise is absolutely crucial to your child's continuing efforts to learn to read.

- If your child is learning to read and asks for a word, give it immediately so that the meaning of the story is not interrupted. DO NOT ask your child to sound out the word.
- On the other hand, if your child initiates the act of sounding out, don't intervene.
- If your child is reading along and makes what is called a miscue, listen for the sense of the miscue. If the word "road" is substituted for the word "street," for instance, no meaning is lost. Don't stop the reading for a correction.
- If the miscue makes no sense (for example, "horse" for "house"), ask your child to reread the sentence because you're not sure you understand what's just been read.
- Above all else, enjoy your child's growing command of print and make sure you give lots of praise. *You are your child's first teacher—and the most important one. Praise from you is critical for further risk-taking and learning.*

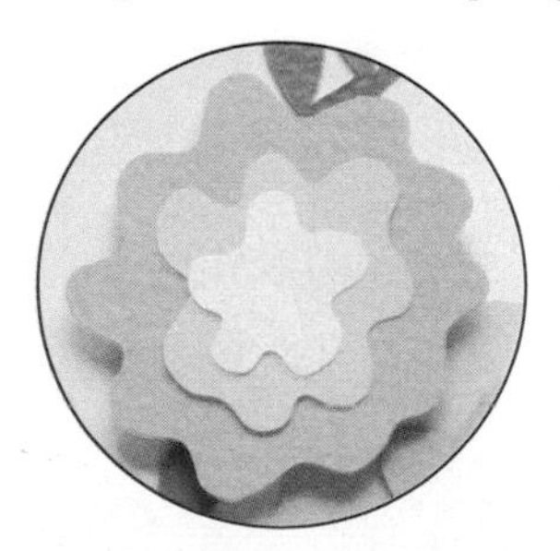

—Priscilla Lynch
Ph.D., New York University
Educational Consultant

For Jordan, who planted the seed of inspiration
—J. Marzollo

For my dear friend, Lugene
—J. Moffatt

Library of Congress Cataloging-in-Publication Data

Marzollo, Jean.
I'm a seed / by Jean Marzollo ; illustrated by Judith Moffatt.
p. cm. — (Hello reader! Level 1)
ISBN 0-590-26586-5
[1. Seeds — Fiction. 2. Pumpkin — Fiction. 3. Flowers — Fiction.] I. Moffatt, Judith, ill. II. Title. III. Series.
PZ7.M3688Iam 1996 95-13237
[E] — dc20 CIP
AC

12 11 10 9 8 7 6 5 4 3 2 1 6 7 8 9/9 0 1/0

Printed in the U.S.A. 23

First Scholastic printing, March 1996

I'm a Seed

by Jean Marzollo
Illustrated by Judith Moffatt

Hello Science Reader!—Level 1

Cartwheel BOOKS®
SCHOLASTIC INC.
New York Toronto London Auckland Sydney

I'm a seed.

I'm a seed, too!

I'm going to be a marigold
when I grow up.

Me, too!

No, you’re not.

Why not?

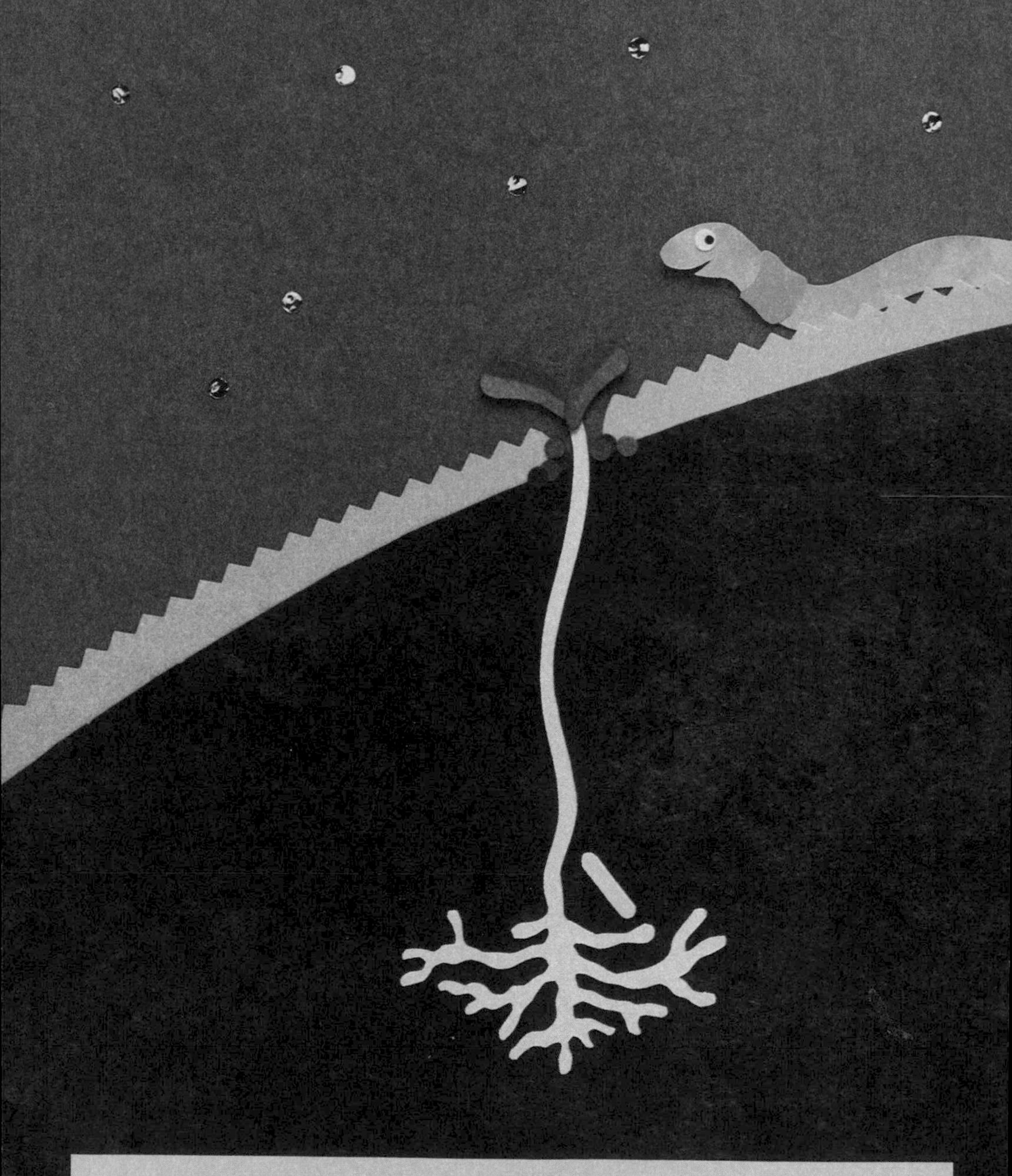

Because you're a
different kind of seed.

What kind of seed am I?

How should I know?
Wait and see.

Wait how long?

Not too long. See?
We're growing.
My stem goes up, up, up.

My stem goes sideways.

My leaves are small and perky.

My leaves are big
and hairy.

My flowers reach up to the sky.

My flowers are hiding under my leaves.

My petals are yellow and orange and frilly.

My petals died.
Now I have green balls!

I have **twenty** flowers!

My green balls turned orange.
What in the world am I?

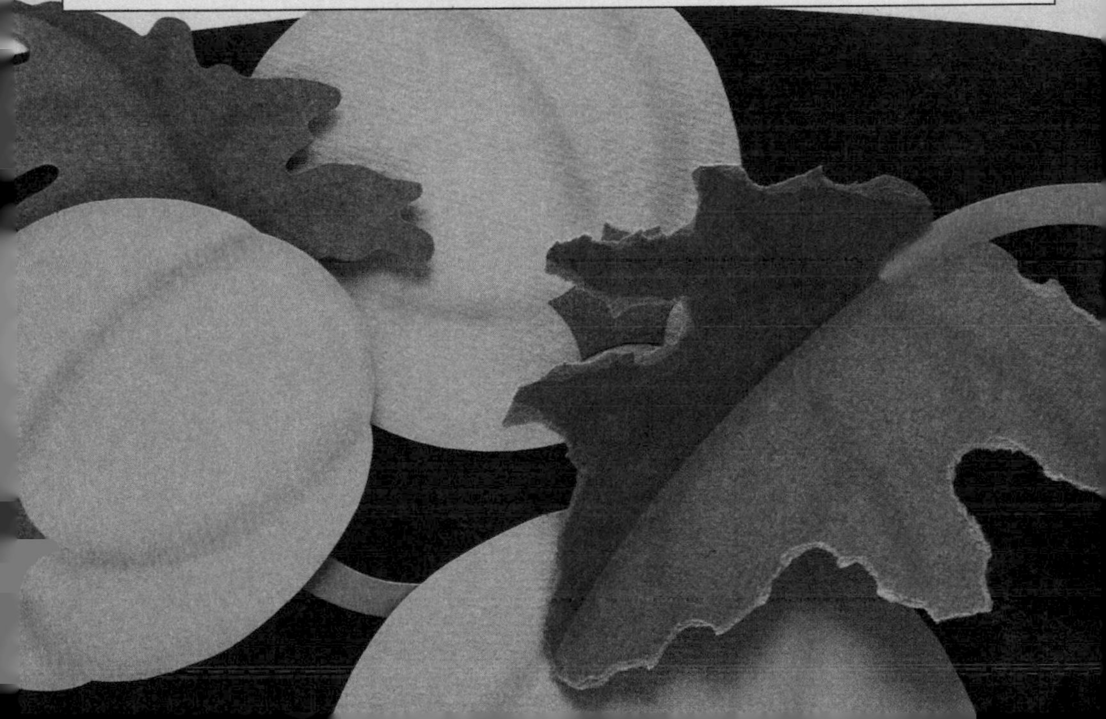

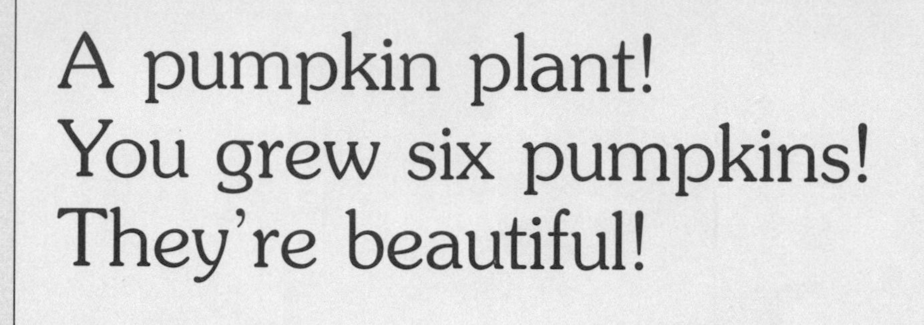

A pumpkin plant!
You grew six pumpkins!
They're beautiful!

Thank you. I am very proud.

Know what's inside of us?

What?

Seeds.
When my seeds are
planted, they will
become new marigolds.

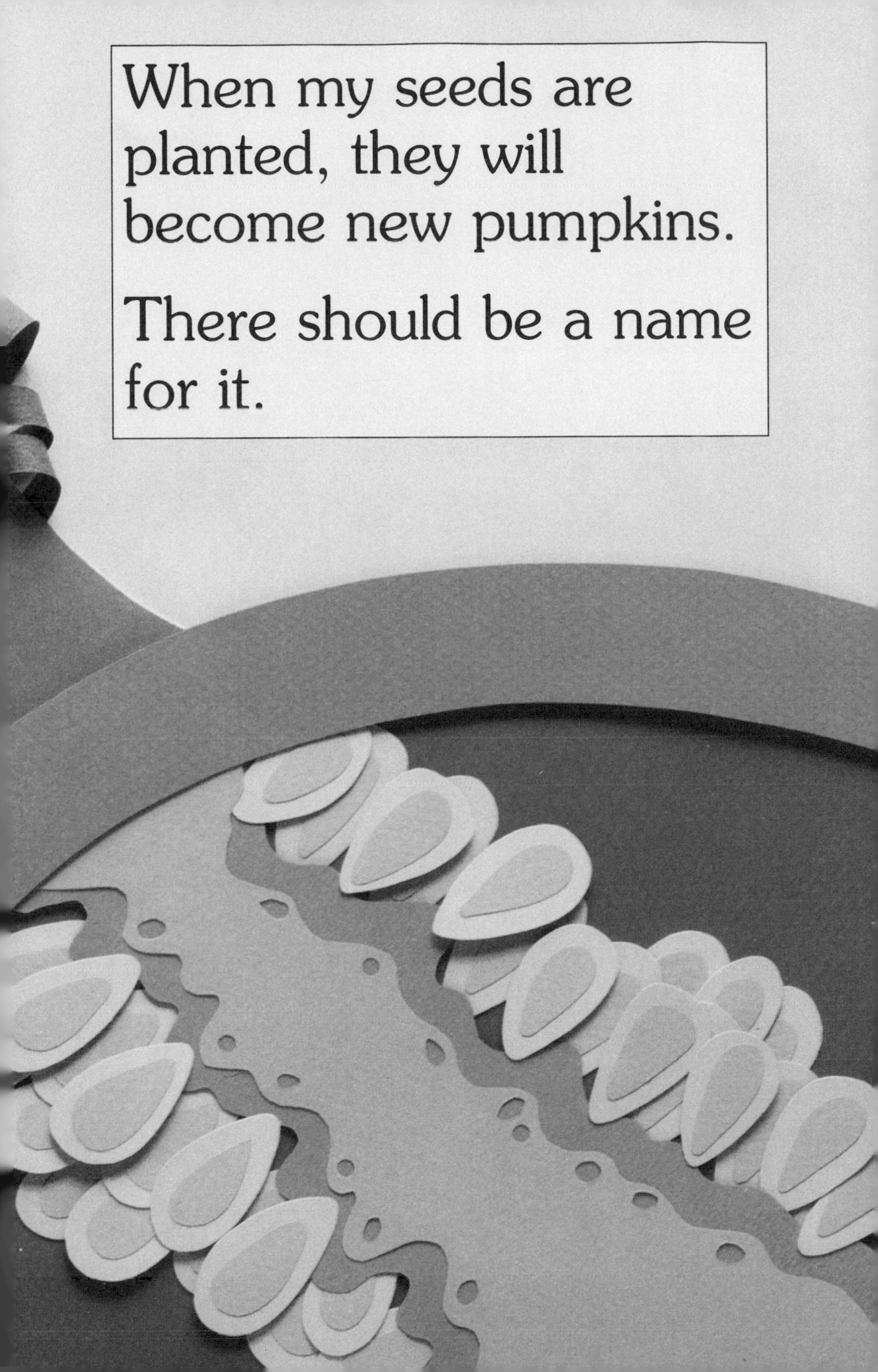

When my seeds are planted, they will become new pumpkins.

There should be a name for it.

There is.
It's called life.